£1.25.

D0490813

MONSTERS
IN MY MAILBOX

By Ellen Jackson   Illustrated by Maxie Chambliss

HINKLER
BOOKS

To Roger Schlueter
—E. J.

Monsters in my mailbox
Published in 2003 by Hinkler Books Pty Ltd
45-55 Fairchild Street
Heatherton Victoria 3202 Australia
www.hinklerbooks.com

10 9 8 7 6 5
10 09 08

In association with BridgeWater Paperback.

Previously published by BridgeWater Paperback, an imprint and
trademark of Troll Communications L.L.C. in 2000.

Text copyright © Lisa McCourt 1999.
Illustrations copyright © Cyd Moore 1999.

978-1-8651-5973 7

Printed and bound in China.

Reginald McGillicuddy lived in a grown-up part of town. Grown-ups lived up the street, down the street, and across the street. And none of them had any children.

No one, that is, except Mr. and Mrs. Applebee next door. They had Anna Marie, who didn't really count because she was a girl.

So Reginald had only his toys to keep him company.

One day Reginald saw an unusual advertisement in a magazine.

"Hmmm," thought Reginald. "I'll join that Monster-of-the-Month Club. Then I'll always have someone to play with."

He shook some money from his piggy bank and mailed it with the coupon. Sure enough, on the first of April, a huge, brown package was delivered to his home.

"What's in the box?" asked Anna Marie, who had been playing hopscotch on the sidewalk.

"Boy stuff," said Reginald as he hauled the package inside. He hoped his parents hadn't seen it. They wouldn't even let him have a kitten.

Reginald opened the box. A blue, furry monster jumped out. "Hello," said the monster. "I'm Stinky."

"Wow!" said Reginald. "You sure are big. What do you eat?"

"Mud pies and box springs," said Stinky. He took a chomp out of Reginald's mattress.

"Let's mix up some mud pies," Reginald quickly said.
Reginald and Stinky loved the monster mud pies.
Reginald's mother did not.

"You need a place to sleep," said Reginald when it was time for bed.

"How about *under* the bed?" said the monster. "I like to snack on dust balls."

So Reginald pushed and shoved and stuffed Stinky under the bed.

With Stinky around, Reginald was never lonely. On the first of May, another package arrived.

"Hello," said Monster Number Two, who was yellow with fangs and wormy hair. "My name is Binky. Gee, it was cramped in that box. You don't happen to have a hot tub I could relax in, do you?"

"You've got to be kidding," said Reginald.

"How about an exercise room or a fax machine?" asked Binky. Reginald shook his head.

"Well, then, I'm leaving," said Binky, stamping his huge foot and smashing a hole through the floor. "I won't belong to some ordinary kid."

"No!" shouted Reginald as Binky headed toward the door. "My folks will see you."

Stinky blocked the door, then pushed Binky into the closet. Reginald slammed the door shut and locked it. Soon they heard Binky gnawing on a shoe.

"Yum. Genuine leather!" said Binky. "I'll sleep here."

With two monster friends, Reginald had twice as much fun, but also twice as much trouble. When the monsters giggled and tickled and rolled on the floor, they smashed Reginald's crayons and kicked over the bookcase.

"Son, I told you not to jump on the bed!" Reginald's dad yelled from downstairs.

"Har! Har! Har!" laughed Stinky. He sounded like a hippopotamus with hiccups.

On the first of June, another monster was delivered.
"Is it your birthday?" called Anna Marie.
"No," said Reginald, closing the front door just in time.

The new monster looked even stranger than the other two. His name was Finky—and he breathed fire.

"It was cold in da box," said Finky. "And I got a runny doze."

Then he coughed and set Reginald's catcher's mitt on fire. Stinky dumped a tray of mud pies on the mitt to put the fire out.

"Don't worry about me," said Finky when it was time for bed. "I'll sleep under the rug."

"Try not to set the house on fire," said Reginald, sighing.

"Look at this room!" said Reginald's mom the next morning. "Get busy, young man. I want you to clean up this mess immediately!"

So Reginald cleaned all day while Stinky, Binky, and Finky lazed around toasting marshmallows.

"Are these my roller skates?" asked Reginald, holding up two gooey, slimy, half-chewed wheels. He was feeling very grumpy.

"Yup!" said Binky with a burp. "The wheels didn't agree with me."

On the first of July, Pinky was delivered, and Ginky arrived in August. Now Reginald had enough monsters for a basketball team. By December, he had a baseball team—until Binky stole and ate all the bases.

By February, the house was chock full of monsters. At night, the old house squeaked and creaked when the monsters were especially twitchy and wiggly.

"Could I have a glass of water?" asked Stinky at midnight.

"Me, too," said Hinky, Rinky, and Linky.

"I want one! I want one!" cried Dinky, Inky, and Shrinky.

"Did you hear that?" Reginald's mother asked his father. "I think we have mice."

On the first of March, a gigantic package was delivered to Reginald's house. Out stepped Monster Number Twelve.

"My name is Winky," said the monster. "I like Ping Pong and pickle sandwiches with ketchup. And I snore."

Reginald and Winky played ninety-eight games of Ping Pong. At bedtime, Reginald put Winky in the coat closet.

"It's too dark in here," said Winky, shivering.
Reginald put Winky in the attic.
"I think I see a spider," said Winky, shuddering. "May I sleep with you? Pretty please?"
"Oh, all right," said Reginald, rolling his eyes.

"Ouch!" said Ginky. "You're squishing me!"

"What was that?" said Winky, sitting up. "Who's there?"

"Me, Banana Brain. I can't breathe," said Ginky, gasping for breath. His white fangs gleamed in the moonlight.

"Don't bite!" screeched Winky, diving out the window.
"My sore toe!" screamed Ginky.

He hopped toward the door and tripped over Finky. Finky jumped up. In his hurry, he mistook the closet door for the exit.

"Help!" he shrieked. "Something big kicked me!"

He let out a blast of fire that singed Binky's wormy hair. Then both monsters screamed and ran through the house to the front door.

The noise scared all the monsters. Shrieking and screaming, they stampeded into the night. Reginald ran after them. In the front yard, the gang of monsters was running amok.

"Oh, no!" groaned Reginald. "What do I do now?"

Anna Marie's window flew open.

"Turn the hose on them!" she shouted.

Without quite knowing why, Reginald grabbed the
garden hose and sprayed the frightened monsters.
    Reginald's father flung open the door. "WHAT ARE
YOU DOING?" he yelled.
    "I...I..." said Reginald helplessly. "I'm watering."

Reginald looked around the yard. All the monsters
had vanished. A swarm of fireflies hovered overhead.
"Well, come in this minute," said Reginald's father.
"That can wait until tomorrow. Goodness, Reginald. What
will you think of next?"

In the morning, Reginald searched everywhere. He couldn't find a single monster.

"Looking for this?" asked a voice.

Reginald looked up to see Anna Marie holding a tiny creature. It was Winky.

"Anna Marie rescued me," said Winky.

"How did you know what to do?" Reginald asked Anna Marie.

"I read the directions," she said, "back when I belonged to the Monster-of-the-Month Club."

"What directions?" Reginald said.

"'If monsters run amok, sprinkle with water,'" said Anna Marie. "'When wet, monsters will shrink, then turn into harmless fireflies.' I dried this one off just in time."

"Anna Marie," said Reginald, "would you like to come over to my house for a nice, quiet game of checkers?"

"If I can bring Zinky," said Anna Marie. She opened her hand. In it was a little monster.

Reginald smiled. "Two monsters sound just right," he said.